WE CAN READ!™

Who Said Boo?

WITHDRAWN

by Jacqueline Sweeney

Photography by G. K. & Vikki Hart
Photo Illustration by Blind Mice Studio

BENCHMARK BOOKS

MARSHALL CAVENDISH
NEW YORK

For two little Boos —
Julian Trester and William Barrett Nunn

With thanks to Daria Murphy, Reading Specialist,
K-8 English Language Arts Coordinator,
for reading this manuscript with care and for writing
the "We Can Read and Learn" activity guide.

Benchmark Books
Marshall Cavendish Corporation
99 White Plains Road
Tarrytown, New York 10591

Text copyright © 2000 by Jacqueline Sweeney
Photo illustrations copyright © 2000 by G. K. & Vikki Hart
and Mark & Kendra Empey

Library of Congress Cataloging-in-Publication Data
Sweeney, Jacqueline.
Who said boo? / Jacqueline Sweeney.
p.   cm. — We can read!
Summary: Animal friends enjoy dressing up in scary Halloween costumes and
going out into the dark night for a party given in Owl Woods.
ISBN 0-7614-0924-6 (lib. bdg.)
[1. Halloween—Fiction. 2. Costume—Fiction. 3. Parties—Fiction. 4.
Animals—Fiction.] I. Title. II. Series: We can read! (Benchmark Books/Marshall
Cavendish)
PZ7.S974255Wh   2000   [E]—dc21 98-47184   CIP   AC

Printed in Italy

1 3 5 6 4 2

Characters

Jim

Tim

Gus

Molly

Ron

Eddie

Ladybug

Hildy

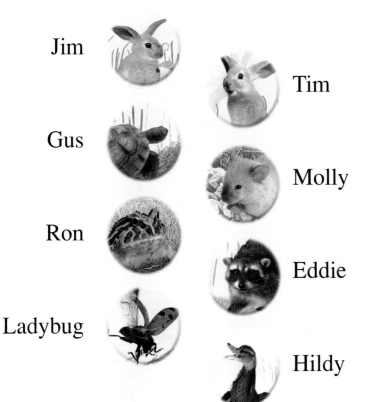

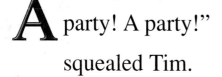

A party! A party!"
squealed Tim.

"Where?" grunted Gus.

"Owl Woods," said Jim.

"And we're all invited."

"It's dark in there!" squeaked Molly.

"Too dark," said Ron.

"Too scary," said Eddie.

"It's supposed to be scary," said Ladybug.
"It's Halloween!"

"We'll need costumes," squeaked Molly.

"I'll surprise you," quacked Hildy.

"I'll scare you," said Eddie.

And off they ran.

Meanwhile,

the owls were busy —

dusting, sweeping,

putting up lights.

The friends met at Pond Rock.
It was dark.
They started walking.

"I'm scared," said Ron.
"Let's hold hands."

"We're here!" squeaked Molly.

"So bright," said Tim.

"It twinkles," said Eddie.

"Oh my," said Jim.

The trees
were filled with
glowing eyes.

"It's time," said Molly,

"to wear a disguise."

The first one in the
clearing was Ladybug.
"I'm an acorn," she said.

"Boo!" came a voice from the dark.

The next one in was Eddie.

"I'm a bear!" he growled.

"Boo!" came a voice from the dark.

"Guess me!" croaked Ron.

"A hawk," quacked Hildy.

She tucked her head under her wing.

"I'm an island," she said.

"Boo!" came a voice from the dark.

"We're a snake," hissed Tim.

Behind him was Jim.

Molly was last.

She was riding on Gus.

"Fairy Princess!"

she said.

"Boo!" came a voice from the dark.

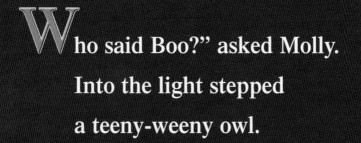

W ho said Boo?" asked Molly.
Into the light stepped
a teeny-weeny owl.

"Who are you?" asked Hildy.
"Boo," said the owl.

Everyone smiled.

"Happy Halloween, Boo," said the friends.

"Happy Halloween!" hooed Boo.

"Boo!" came a voice from the dark.

WE CAN READ AND LEARN

The following activities are designed to enhance literacy development. *Who Said Boo?* can help children to build skills in vocabulary, phonics, and creative writing; to explore self-awareness; and to make connections between literature and other subject areas such as science and math.

BOO'S CHALLENGE WORDS

Using the words listed below, children and adults can take turns telling a scary story. One person begins the story, and each person continues until it reaches a spine-tingling conclusion!

acorn	bear	clearing	disguise
glow	growl	grunt	hawk
island	scare	snake	surprise
tuck	twinkle	woods	

FUN WITH PHONICS

You can play Boo! and also help children practice phonics skills for short a and short u words. Use white index cards or plain white paper to cut out ghostly shapes. On each "ghost" write a short a or short u word chosen from the list below. Make a duplicate set of ghosts. Distribute cards between two to four players. Each player asks the next player to match a word or vowel sound. If a match is made, the player who asked for the match gets the ghost. The first player to match all his or her ghosts calls out "boo!" The other players can continue until all their ghosts have disappeared.

Short a words:

and	an
ran	last
at	asked
hands	happy

Short u words:

Gus	grunted
up	dusting
under	supposed
tucked	ladybug

30

WHO REALLY DID SAY BOO?

Have children write a new ending to solve the mystery of who said "boo!" Re-read the ending aloud. Discuss possibilities with children, adding a few rhyming words to each new ending. (Try boo, hoo, too, you, who.)

When the new endings are written and ready to share, children can make and wear special Boo glasses to help them read. To make Boo glasses, you need one sheet of 9 X 12 construction paper for each child, preferably white, and a tongue depressor or stick to stir paint. Create large bubble letters that spell BOO! Cut out and glue or tape each side to the sticks. Children can read their stories "boo . . . tifully!"

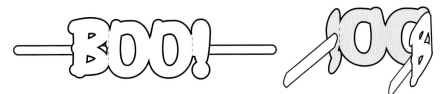

YOU'RE INVITED!

The characters in *Who Said Boo?* were invited to a Halloween party. Children can design an invitation and have a real or pretend party. They can invite friends, family members, or even stuffed animals. Invitations should say why the party is being given, the place, the time, and to whom to respond. Invitations can be individually decorated and then delivered to friends, family, or stuffed animal pals. It can even be a costume party, whether or not it's Halloween.

ROLE PLAY

Who Said Boo? is a dramatic story. Have children take turns playing different parts, acting out the story in their own words or reading their parts from the book, just like reading from a script. Props such as costumes or pretend trees can make the story come alive.

OWL WOODS RESEARCHERS

Owl Woods got its name because it is a home for many owls. There are lots of types, or species, of owls: barn owls, burrowing owls, spotted owls, and great horned owls, to name a few. Children can visit their school or local library to gather facts about owls. Where do owls nest? Which is the smallest owl? When do owls sleep? What is special about the way an owl's eyes move and work?

Have children record their findings by writing each fact on a paper tree and then gluing the trees to a large sheet of paper. They create their own Owl Woods of facts. Illustrations of each owl can be placed in the woods.

About the author

Jacqueline Sweeney has published children's poems and stories in many anthologies and magazines. An author for Writers in the Schools and for Alternative Literary Programs in Schools, she has written numerous professional books on creative methods for teaching writing. She lives in Stone Ridge, New York.

About the photo illustrations

The photo illustrations are the collaborative effort of photographers G. K. and Vikki Hart and Blind Mice Studio. Following Mark Empey's sketched story board, G. K. and Vikki Hart photograph each animal and element individually. The images are then scanned and manipulated, pixel by pixel, by Mark and Kendra Empey at Blind Mice Studio.

Each charming illustration may contain from 15 to 30 individual photographs.

All the animals that appear in this book were handled with love. The ladybugs and butterflies were set free in the garden, while the others have been returned to or adopted by loving homes.